WE NEVER GO OUT OF
STYLE

TANZANIA GLOVER

embodied in critical reviews and certain other noncommercial uses permitted by copyright law. This book or any portion thereof may not be reproduced or used in any manner without the express written permission of the writer or publisher. The use of brief quotations is allowed in book reviews.

Cover art by Sia Tania of Design Boutique NL

Www.tanzaniaglover.com

JP!!! I literally couldn't have done this without you and I can't thank you enough for being gracious enough to help fill in the gaps in my brain where fashion knowledge is supposed to be. You're the best!

FASHION KILLA

I used to live to make an entrance. In fact, once upon a time the only thing I loved more than being fashionably late was just plain old being fashionable, but these days I had more important things on my mind.

The usually formidable Penny Pope had been a bad little stylist lately, but through it all Mikel had been the most patient, gentle and forgiving agent I could ask for in the last nine years of my decade-long career. And I'd gone and broken his heart with one single word: no.

No, I wasn't ready to style somebody again.

No, I still wasn't ready to face people or their questions.

And no, I certainly wasn't up to dealing with a high-maintenance piece of work like Easton "Do you know who my parents are?" Woods.

However, that *No* must've been the straw that broke Mikel's perfectly gym-toned back because he suddenly rolled out a few *Nos* of his own, the funniest being, "No Penny, actually I heard Easton is a joy to work with, but even if he's not it's still time to get your big country ass off that farm and back to civilization."

I smiled thinking back on his words again before remembering that there was actually one *Yes* in his very blunt email. It was, "And yes, you'd best be looking for another agent if you don't accept this job because this pathetic mourning period over a man of all things has to come to an end immediately, Stinkabutt. I'm sending love with your boarding pass."

And as much as I didn't like it, he wasn't wrong about any of it. If Mikel was at the end of his patience with me then I'd definitely gone too far especially since he had even enlisted my timorous assistant Denise to call to drive some sense into my head.

"Penny, Easton's agent specifically called and asked to work with you. That's a really big deal and I think you should do it," she said before revealing the true motivation behind her sudden bout of pushiness. "Because who knows when I'll ever get another opportunity to find out if Big Easy really is big and easy?!" she exclaimed, but I barely heard her exposed libido over her former words.

"Wait he's one of Teegan's clients? And she had the balls to let my name come out of her mouth?" I asked through nearly bared teeth because just thinking about her instantly put me on edge.

Being well-connected had kept her from being hung out to dry with the rest of the women in my ex Jake's cheating exposé from the year before, but I still remembered seeing her texts and pictures in his phone. And I'd made no qualms about letting her know that I knew.

"I know! I know! But we don't have to work with her directly. Just Easton. And maybe this is her way of trying to make amends with you?"

The suggestion that Teegan Ravin could be apologetic about anything she had done to me was about as ludicrous as Christopher Brian Bridges, but I would never be mean enough to tell Denise that. Especially since ultimately I knew I would have to take the job anyway because I couldn't dare lose Mikel.

So there I was tossing my favorite plaid flannel into the laundry basket so that I could put on some ridiculously expensive sweater that had been gifted by a designer a few seasons ago. The black cashmere was soft and lovely, high quality cashmere always was, but it didn't have the same charm as my black and red shirt.

Was it too soon to bring plaid back again?

I mean I'd personally never stopped wearing it at home, but surely more than enough time had passed since the Great Plaid Invasion of twenty-thirteen a decade ago. I started mulling a potential shoot with a faceless model in my head. It could work. Maybe plaid with lace and leather, a *Mary Poppins* meets punk moment? Hm.

I jumped at the soft knock on my door harder than I needed to which made my sister Simone smile.

"Ready to get back to the runway?"

"Not even close. All day I've been praying to our lord and savior Tim Gunn to give me strength and guide me through."

Still amused by our old *Project Runway* jokes, she let herself in then leaned against the door to my more often than not Pennyless bedroom.

"Your mama and daddy said they're not going to bed no matter how late you plan on leaving. Her exact words were, 'Tell Penelope Ann to get her big butt downstairs and say goodbye like she's got some sense.'"

"Damn Mikel was just talking about my booty too. Has it really gotten that big?" I asked quickly standing to look at myself from behind in the full-length mirror.

Sitting around and eating whatever I wanted for my year off had done wonders for my mental health, but I already knew it would take me a hot, country minute to get back into the sample sizes I'd gotten accustomed to fitting into.

"Yeah it's almost got its own orbit," she cracked and I shot her a look because she had practically been born bootylicious. Mama too. "Okay don't even start. I don't feel like having to tussle with you before you leave."

"We'll have plenty of time for that again when I get back," I said as I playfully mushed her since despite being the closest we still argued more than anybody else did too.

Noting the time I quickly tossed the last of my things into my suitcase then closed up shop. It was basically just new underwear and toiletries since I had an entire wardrobe in storage in London. I'd worked with countless UK starlets over the years so it had almost become like a second home.

"So hopefully I'll be back in time to help, but in case I'm not please don't slack helping Daddy with the spring planting. No excuses. We need to be ready for summer so don't be lazy and cut any corners."

"Don't you think that would be better directed at Max?" she asked with a sly smirk about our oldest sister who pretty much had a hall pass for as long as she needed.

I told her with my eyes not to play with me about Max because my big sister had been through enough to never have to work again if she didn't want to. Thankfully after that she dropped the issue and instead picked up Cayenne, the small, brown stuffed horse she'd given me years ago as a birthday gift. Her work-roughened fingers stroked his careworn yarn mane just like she did with her old piebald.

"You really think you'll be home again that quick? I figured you would be gone at least 'til June."

"Oh no. I will not be following Easton Woods around

until this summer. I don't have the patience and plus real Cayenne will miss me if I'm gone that long." Ugh just thinking about being away from my horse again made me even sadder. "You swear you'll take good care of my baby? Work her out every day? Give her my special treats?"

"Of course I will. You know you don't have to worry about that. Just do your work so we can get you home and finish up these last fixes on the retreat. That's all I want. Oh and you could try to wear something, *anything* that's not black for a change. We don't want Easton thinking you worship the Devil like that Christian singer you used to style," she laughed out, but I was still not in the mood to join her.

"He'd better thank his lucky stars that I'm blessing him with my presence in the first place, how about that? Now come give me some love."

As I grabbed her in for one final big embrace, I stifled a huge scream deep inside my chest. My wound-licking solitude period had obviously come to an end and my career was demanding its due at long last. With luck Easton Woods would fall in line and I'd be on a plane back to Illinois before spring was over.

I prayed like hell that the Cali boy actor would be nothing more than a small bump in the road to my future because just like Max, I had been through enough too.

...

While on the long overnight flight from O'Hare to Heathrow I decided to finally do my due diligence and research Big Easy as Denise and the press sometimes called him because of his height and other *things* he'd gotten a reputation for. Typically I did my deep dive long before meeting my clients, but I had put this one off until the very last minute hoping Mikel came to his senses and didn't actually make me do it. But since he had, the time had come for me to find out exactly how big of a diva I would be dealing with for the foreseeable future.

As the son of two big-time directors, Earl Woods and Evelyn Sturkey, there had always been buzz around him and his fellow actor and twin sister Elly. Evelyn had been a global phenom as a runway model before Earl famously took her to some distant island getaway for their first date and won her over.

Apparently it took years of trying, but he managed to impress her so much that by the time they resurfaced again they were wedded and pregnant with Eleanor Rose and Earl Easton Woods Jr. Whoever had decided to brand them as Elly and Easton had made a great call because not even their beautiful faces could overcome those Bible Belt, Great Depression names.

And although he actually seemed like a pretty smart guy in interviews, he had shamelessly leaned on those boyish good looks and parlayed them into an unprecedented run of romantic comedy roles. However, according to Mikel's briefing those kind of roles weren't enough to contain his talent and Easton Woods longed to become the next up-and-coming serious Tinseltown wonder. Insert eyeroll here.

I saw that he had also been keeping busy with modeling because why not exploit nepotism in both of his parents' industries, right? I hadn't had the misfortune of seeing any of his movies yet, but I did have to admit he was a half decent model as I looked from magazine cover to editorial and marveled at his range and versatility.

He basically looked good in everything, from goofy avant-garde designs to urban Japanese streetwear. Yet in his free time he seemed to mostly rock the standard American male uniform: jeans, sneakers and a hoodie. Literally every single pap shot was in a goddamned hoodie and jeans.

I clicked another picture with bated breath just knowing I was wrong about what was hanging from his back, but my first scan was right on the money and I knew then that this would be a bigger struggle than I'd initially thought. The man had actually worn a hoodie underneath a tuxedo jacket. It all suddenly made sense why Teegan had decided to swallow her pride to reach out since she knew that not many others were capable of pulling off the kind of miracle needed in his case.

Finally I decided that my eyes had been tortured enough by his styling being an afterthought for so long so I looked over his event schedule. He was finishing up some reshoots in a "colorblind casting" World War II film for the few weeks or so. There was also an editorial spread and interview in Heritage magazine, a couple of fashion show appearances and some press junkets. Nobody had said a thing about award season and I certainly wasn't going to mention it or worry about it since my end goal was to get done then get back home.

By the time I arrived in London I was bleary-eyed and rumpled and my memory had obviously reset and wiped away every vestige of my old jet-setting life. Like the spoiled little starlets that I had worked with throughout the years I'd nearly forgotten how tedious it was to fly commercial.

My ex and biggest mistake, Jake, had avoided regular passenger flights like the plague because of course when you're handsome, rich and self-centered how could you be expected to mix with the common people? As one of pro hockey's most well-known and highly paid players and born into one of those "old money" families, he lived a life of complete luxury that I never imagined until I got serious with him years ago.

Simone was a great judge of character and had warned me about him from the start, but I was notoriously hard headed and hadn't listened. I'd learned the hard way though and had the emotional scars to prove it.

After mentally checking out of the not-so-distant past then into the hotel, I decided to call up my wardrobe storage service to get some of my more glam and fashionable clothes delivered to me. It would be anybody's guess whether anything fit anymore, but I wasn't about to drop thousands on new pieces because it wasn't my job to be the focus of attention after all. That was all on Earl Easton.

My phone buzzed as I finished up the last of my clothing arrangements. It was Denise, but I could hardly hear her over the airport din.

"It's been so hard to get around today. I don't know if it's mercury retrograde or what, but I almost missed my plane this morning. I'll be there as soon as I can, alright?"

"Take your time. I'm just looking at some pieces that I might pull tomorrow. My plan is to stay under the radar and take it easy for the next few weeks."

"Small chance of that with London Fashion Week starting in a few days and I hear some of the menswear designers are already showing."

"Tell me about it. When I was calling my favorite showrooms I hinted around that I probably wouldn't be able to make it to anything, but they all literally said they're still sending invites," I complained and swore I could hear her smile on the other end before she spoke.

"Good. We need to officially get you back to your old self anyway and this is the only way to do it."

Just then an email alert popped up in my phone notifications from none other than Mikel.

Penny,

I've accepted a couple RSVPs on your behalf. Not enough to mess up you and Denise's schedule too much, but just enough so that people see that stunning face and know you're back in business. Touch base with me in a couple days.

Mikel

I flopped back on the bed and stared at the ceiling. This was a cursed day and the only way to break it was through sleep so that's exactly what I did.

The nap and reflection brought me to my senses. Mama and Daddy would've had a fit over all the griping I'd been doing. I could almost hear him now, always sensible and no-nonsense, "Well give the free clothes and party invites to somebody who'll appreciate them and come haggle over corn seed with us instead."

He would've been right too. Besides I was here now so it was time for me to stop acting like a pouting little baby and get back to work. I was lucky to have a job that many people would kill to do and also get paid handsomely for.

Without it there was no way I would have been able to save enough to build something with my sisters that would be able to help others for years to come with our retreat. I needed to count my blessings and hit this out of the ballpark just like I'd always done.

Denise got to work the second she arrived which made me feel like a complete slacker since I hadn't bothered doing much of anything aside from twiddling my thumbs while I waited for her to arrive. I loved the sound that her freshly done nails made as they tapped against the keyboard. She was busy entering some of the packed slate of events into the calendar, but I didn't realize just how packed they were until she read them aloud.

"Let me just confirm. Tomorrow at eight is the Halpern show, Cortili at ten, L.Y.P.H. at three then Burberry at seven. You have an appointment to pull garments at Industrial at noon and another at Affiliated Pieces at five. Industrial and Affiliated will then send the pieces to Gambit Studios Thursday. Do I have that right?"

I did one more scan of my notes to make sure I hadn't missed anything, but I had been enjoying her nail music so much that I'd missed a couple things.

"Don't forget to remind Marina at Affiliated to pull those accessories and shoes that I picked and if you could call up Cartier and that awesome watch shop for some items, that would be good too."

"Okay, will do. Did Teegan tell you anything else about the Heritage photo shoot?"

"Well they've got a couple of objectives here. The theme is World War II but modernized, you know? Maybe a dandy type thing for one shot then a country suit or a rakish look with some leather. They only requested five, but we should pull enough clothes for at least eight looks."

"That sounds interesting. Cortili will definitely have something for us, especially with all their nice wool plaids and structural features," she threw in and I noted that she was finally giving her suggestions without me having to pull it out of her first. The year break had done us both some good and she was well on her way to being a great stylist in her own right soon.

I sighed thinking about how all of our beautiful hard work was about to be wasted on somebody who probably wouldn't even keep it up when he wasn't being forced into it. It was a shame too because imagining him in well-tailored sophisticated clothing was just about as appealing as imagining him in nothing, but I quickly shook my head to rid me of those kinds of thoughts.

"Denise, do you know he wore a hoodie under a tux jacket to a movie premiere? His last stylist must've had a fit."

"Well I heard they didn't have much time for styling if you catch my drift," she offered before trying to move on, but I kindly asked her to elaborate since Easton nor his previous stylist Jade Baker had been on my radar. Plus I'd been out of the loop for too long now so I needed to start catching up on my behind the scenes gossip anyway.

It was far from anything truly salacious though. Apparently they had just dated on and off for a while, but it ended because he wasn't ready to settle down which partially explained all the terrible clothing decisions as of late.

"How long ago was that? I didn't see any pictures of them on my search and I saw him with plenty of women."

"Maybe around the same time you broke up with Jerk," she said like she was trying to show some restraint, but her voice still dripped with disapproval

"Oh, that's his name now?" I asked amused and again loving this new Denise who said exactly what was on her mind.

"Well I'd rather call him something else, but I'm on the clock. And if you don't mind me saying you look like you're healing up well after him though."

"Thanks, but you don't have ro do that. I won't melt into a puddle of undignified goo if I hear Jake's name, I swear."

After three years together I still hurt some, but the memory wasn't as much of a stabbing thrust to the gut as it had been when everything first exploded in my face.

We worked until my clothes arrived from the storage unit. Seeing all the bags was so weird, like I'd stuffed some old friends in a closet and done my best to forget they existed, but I really missed this. As ridiculous as fashion could be sometimes, there was just something magical about being on set for a shoot or backstage at a show.

The rush of creating a visual story with textiles and metals was intoxicating. I could get drunk off of beauty of all sorts be it art, fabric or men. The latter had gotten me into more trouble than I cared to admit though, but it was okay. I was surrounded by something that I loved and I would let nothing take that away from me again.

I became so engrossed in reacquainting myself with my clothes—oh that was where my Stuart Weitzman boots had gotten to!—that I jumped at the knock on my bedroom door.

"Hey, Penny, just to let you know, Easton's assistant Amal

invited us for drinks tonight. Do you want me to accept?"

My stomach did a two second tango. My return to styling had been all talk until I actually had to face a client again in the flesh. I couldn't exactly turn back now so I shrugged.

They wanted to meet up at Electric House in Notting Hill at seven. It was just after five so I had just enough time to pull myself together. I was one of the best in the game and Easton Woods, America's pretty boy thespian, was paying top dollar for my work. I had nothing to fear. It was my time again.

...

Electric House teemed with industry types that night. Don't ask me how I'd forgotten it was fashion week when I'd been working around fashion events the whole day, but I had somehow neglected to put two and two together. But I guess that running into all the people I had purposely been avoiding for the past year because they were all taking Jake's side anyway could be fun.

Luckily Amal had reserved a private nook for the four of us, but having to walk through a sea of people to get to it kind of defeated the purpose. It was time to play the classic game of "If I can't see them, they can't see me," also known as staring down at the floor or straight ahead with tunnel vision. The tactic had failed me countless times when I was a girl and hadn't wanted to muck out the stable, but I was still willing to try and try again.

I barely made it two feet before hearing, "Oh my god! Penny, Is that you?!"

I winced. It was Clarence Jordan, the style editor for Vogue UK. He'd been one of my friends but like others had seemed awfully shady when the Jake shenanigans went down so I'd left him behind with everybody else when I'd gone on hiatus.

Denise gave me a pitying look that said she would save me if I wanted her to, but I shook my head since there wasn't any way around these long overdue meetings. It would still be a trial by fire for sure though.

I turned around and instantly found myself drowning in man chest with two thick arms clasped around me. To say I was shocked would be an understatement especially since the two-cheek kiss was the classic fashion greeting of choice. A hug actually meant something real.

He backed up then smiled down at me from his lofty height of well over six feet. His perfectly cut gray check suit and wire-rimmed glasses made him look like the centerfolds he styled and his locs were longer with a touch more gray than the last time I'd seen him. Time had stood still on the farm but obviously not in the rest of the world.

"Where have you been?" Clarence asked surveying me with the patented stylist once-over. "Here or New York hasn't been the same without you."

In fashion so many people didn't tell the truth so I made it a point to do exactly that whenever I could.

"*Home* home. I needed to get my act together and take a break, you know?"

"I can imagine. Fucking Jake. Let me tell you, the things I said to that man after I saw that article in the Daily Mail. I didn't even want to say anything because you like to keep such a low profile, but I made him regret his life for a minute."

Hearing that made me let out a breath that I'd been holding for more than a year.

"Wait. Is that why you were acting so weird after things went down?"

"Yes, of course. I really just didn't know what to say. Then you vanished and I thought I'd really messed up. I should've just come clean. I missed you, Penny."

"Clarence," I replied very quietly, "I owe you a very long phone call. I thought...you know what, never mind what I thought. I'm happy you found me tonight, okay?"

He looked like I'd given him a million dollars and I felt something blossom in me. I was starting to feel okay. Not perfect, but okay. That had been the missing piece, the thing that Jake had murdered with his carelessness. Maybe I'd feel safe again eventually, but I was good with okay for now.

I was just about to reach for Clarence to give him another hug when there was a tap on my shoulder.

"Sorry Denise. I was just talking to my old friend here," I said putting emphasis on *friend* as I turned around. "Have you met--"

I wasn't talking to Denise. Instead I faced what was probably the most disarmingly attractive man I'd ever seen. He knocked me so off kilter, in fact, that all I could do was stare.

So *this* was Easton Woods in the flesh.

From my vantage point the hype was completely justified. It was literally **distracting**, *disturbing* and just downright <u>disrespectful</u> how he managed to look even better standing in front of me than he did in pictures.

"No, I haven't," he replied, grinning wickedly after a second too long of being ogled. "I'm also not named Denise, but for you I think I would pretty much answer to anything."

"Uh yes. Ahem." Why didn't I have something to drink? My mouth and tongue were unable to work all the sudden. "You must be Easton Woods?"

"Yeah and you must be the beautiful Penelope Pope I've heard so much about," he replied after turning the hundred watt smile down to a seventy-five.

"She prefers Penny," Clarence interjected, his raised eyebrow taunting me over the rim of his glass as he took a sip.

"I do and this is Clarence Jordan, the style editor of Vogue UK," I said going on autopilot as I looked around for Denise because it really was time for a drink now.

Still several feet away but within eyesight, she looked like she was busy coordinating something other than event schedules with a handsome Middle Eastern man who I assumed was Easton's assistant Amal. Go Denise!

Easton's laugh was easy and rich as he shook Clarence's outstretched hand and briefly talked about an editorial he'd shot with him before. It was a real snoozer, but when in doubt I decided I'd depend on my politesse to get me through.

"Well Clarence, it was so great to see you again, but we're gonna go and discuss some upcoming events I'm styling for Easton. Maybe we can grab a bite this week?"

Always a gentleman who knew when to take his leave, he encouraged me to "Jump On It" with his eyes before turning his nose up at the eager room of social climbers.

Uncomfortable at the slowly mounting attention we were getting, I started to walk towards our private nook, but Easton stopped me.

"Hey do you want anything to drink? I was about to get something."

"Um, yes, that would be great. I'll take a Guinness on tap."

"Good pick. You have great taste."

"Maybe. That could change. I might still dress you in some avant-garde tent or something, you know?" I said half-seriously because now I was curious about what item of clothing he wouldn't naturally flatter.

"No, I know I'm in good hands. Teegan wouldn't have recommended you if that wasn't the case."

"Keep thinking that. I'm storyboarding stilts and freakishly long leather gloves. It'll be a concept for the ages."

His perfect forehead crinkled a bit.

"I think I can see where you're going. It's a statement about the heights of fashion and style and how one can transcend them to start a successful dramatic acting career, right?"

His silliness was so unexpected that I chuckled. He was a charmer for sure, I noted as that sinful little half-smile flashed again.

"We're getting to the point pretty quickly, I see."

"Yeah I don't like wasting time. You'll find out," he added suggestively causing my tummy to flip again.

Our little room was located near the bar with one of the large wooden doors half shut to give us some privacy. I snuggled into the mustard yellow armchair and sipped the drink that the server had just dropped off. Now that things had quieted down I was able to finally relax a bit and start talking about my plan and vision for the weeks to come.

For about an hour the four of us discussed objectives, travel arrangements and other things I'd need to know heading into our work together. Easton and Amal seemed to be as tight a team as Denise and I and I was excited to work with somebody so eager to just sit back and let me do my thing.

The familiar rush started to take over the more I imagined this beautiful creature in my hand-picked outfits. The longer I looked at him the surer I was that no man deserved to have such lush, thick eyelashes like he did. Plus he had that sort of muscular yet spare body that no woman I knew would ever kick out of bed.

He looked like a farm boy gone Beverly Hills bad and I was going to mold him into everybody's down-home prince. By the time I was done with him he'd be the only name in Oscars contention, every bit the charismatic and mature Hollywood man.

Denise finished entering the final notes on her phone then started to gather her things. As Amal followed her lead I realized that Easton had told his assistant to go home too in an attempt at alone time with me. Before they could get out the door I asked Denise to wait up as casually as I could, but my heart started to prance Cayenne-style in my chest when I saw the sexy but still disappointed look on his face when he realized I wouldn't be staying.

Yes a few things on this trip would be a smidge different from how I'd planned, but I would keep tight control of at least one: I was not going to get caught up in the web that Easton Woods was famous for spinning.

Already his nearly unbreakable eye contact and pleasantries more than hinted that there was interest there, but I knew I couldn't let myself be too flattered by it. A very handsome one he was, but at the end of the day he was still just a man and just this once I would make sure that my *pinky* listened to my brain.

LONDON BRIDGE

Penny Pope was officially back like she never left! I knew the shoot would be one for the books, but it had already been going even better than expected. Since the story was about Easton's evolution from comedic heartthrob to serious actor, I'd selected well-cut suits in interesting colors, crisp button down shirts and bright, striking accessories.

I'd aimed to bridge his familiar all-American streetwear look with a more upbeat, playful take on the society gent and I'd succeeded in the best way. The sample shots were some of the best I'd seen and any could have easily been a cover shot with the colors popping against his perfectly sunkissed skin and toned body.

As I directed the assistants who were sorting away the clothes and accessories for return, Molly, Heritage magazine's editor-at-large, came over and beckoned me to the side.

"Penny, I have to say this shoot is stunning. Easton looks fantastic and it's such a different vibe for him. I'm living for it!" she exclaimed trying to sound younger than her cute all gray bob would allow her to.

"Thank you! That means a lot coming from you, Molly."

She took my hands in hers and looked me dead in the eye. "It's good to have you back and don't be a stranger, you hear me? We need you and I'll be in touch for more work soon."

I smiled to myself as I counted shoes almost missing that we were short one pair. I did a quick look around but didn't see them.

"Hey," I said to one of the wardrobe assistants walking by, "Did you happen to see another pair of brown shoes?"

"Oh yeah," he said motioning towards Easton's dressing room. "Denise said you wanted us to leave all the remainders in the dressing room, right?"

He was right. I thanked him then headed that way still on a high from Molly's kind words.

"Easton? You decent?" I asked after a polite knock.

"Am I ever?" Cute.

"Are you decent enough so that I can come in?" I added specifically because I seemed to lose all semblance of togetherness around him when fully clothed so I knew I'd probably drool if he was in anything less.

"Penny, get in here!" he playfully demanded as he swung the door open for me. "It's nothing you and the rest of the world hasn't already seen anyway."

"Right. Sorry to interrupt, but I left some extra sh--"

I looked up and literally choked on my words. For the second time since I'd been in London I was faced with man chest, but this one was vastly different from Clarence's. Easton offered a glorious, muscular chest and abs, tapering down into a pair of unbuttoned dress pants and some very low-riding briefs.

I'd been raised Catholic but never was much of a churchgoer, but this man was singlehandedly proving that god made no mistakes.

Even worse? Attempting to walk to get to the shoes I'd spotted after prying my eyes away from his beautiful body, I'd lost my balance so of course when he went to catch me, my hands landed smack dab flat onto his bare pecs. *Geez.*

My eyes flew upwards into his as he stared down at me and I suddenly couldn't move. Time had stopped. There was no studio outside, just me and him in this little room, his heart beating under my increasingly warm hand. I had to breathe and return to reality.

"I am so so sorry." My mouth was suddenly dry and my tongue tied into knots again. He just grinned as I regained composure and stood upright again.

"Don't be. I actually need you to close the door then touch me some more," he said purposely trying to sound cheeky before elaborating. "I don't have a dresser to finish the shoot so if you don't mind I could use your help."

It took me a second to really take in what he'd said. Of course, my lady bits had processed his words instantly, which led to immediate tingling and some really inappropriate thoughts, but when the meaning became crystal clear I snapped myself out of my horny haze.

"What do you mean, you don't have a dresser? I sent Chad back here to--oh, wait. He's putting clothes away."

Denise wasn't even on set because she was pulling clothes for another event so there was no one else left.

"Well, it's your lucky day. I'm your only option."

Pulling on the button-down that I'd selected he casually said, "I'm in good hands, then," but about a quarter of my misshapen coal lump of a heart melted in that moment.

I had to step back a little to get some air, trying to look at anything else but his adept, slender fingers buttoning his shirt.

"There was a tie with this outfit, right? Let me grab the tie."

After reluctantly shutting the door I played around with the cool fabric and let the purple silk slip through my fingers as a distraction until he cleared his throat to get my attention.

"Oh. Sorry. Here you go." I reached out, tie in hand, waiting for him to take it, but he didn't.

"You're not going to believe this, but I actually suck at tying ties."

"Well you can't wear a tie with a hoodie so it makes sense," I said allowing myself to feel just a touch superior for a second before mumbling, "But I'm sure you've probably tried to."

"Sorry I didn't catch that," he said but instead of repeating myself I practically had a stylist meltdown just thinking of his disaster of a hoodie-tux again.

"Easton, what the hell were you thinking wearing that to a movie premiere?!"

When it finally dawned on him what he was being accosted for his eyes fell down as he stifled a laugh.

"C'mon it was a vibe!" he weakly defended.

"It was an eyesore is what it was and if I ever catch you in something like that again you will regret it for the rest of your life!" I threatened before we both finally erupted into a fit of laughter.

"Okay. Okay. I, Easton Woods, solemnly swear now that I've met my lucky Penny thar I'll never wear a hoodie on a red carpet again," he promised as his eyes sparkled with sneaky mischief.

His lucky Penny? Oh he was good at this.

I pretended not to even hear that part though and resumed my task of tying his tie. He had bent so that I wouldn't be on my tip toes so we were nearly face to face when he almost worriedly came back with, "Wait I can still wear them to other events though, right?"

"No, no and no." I bit my lip as I finished up the particular knot that I wanted for this look. "Easton a hoodie is for hanging out. It's the thing you grab off the floor when you wake up and need to throw something on."

"Ah you're one of those then?" he asked amused as he checked himself out in the full-length mirror and preened slightly.

"One of what?"

"A hoodie thief," he accused like they were the bane of his existence as I playfully rolled my eyes and hoped that I wasn't blushing too hard.

"Definitely not."

"You sure? I bet you could accessorize the hell out of one of my hoodies and actually make it a vibe," he said forwardly.

Oh he wasn't even trying to fight fair.

I was in trouble.

The rest of the shoot was pretty uneventful but still took a lot longer than I'd expected. By the time we wrapped up it was close to dinnertime and all I could think about was resting my feet and having a nice, big pint of beer somewhere.

But first I had to do a final check on all the borrowed pieces then I needed to touch base with Easton about our next few events. One was an upcoming press hit for the movie and he was also planning to attend a few fashion shows, some of the same ones I'd been invited to.

As I went to knock on the door again I had to ground myself.

No, I couldn't give into what I was feeling, no matter what.

No, I couldn't let him pull me in with his witty comebacks and happy, shiny eyes.

And no, I certainly wasn't about to become part of the official Easton Woods list of female conquests.

God was with me this time because he was dressed in a pair of selvage Levi's, Margiela sneakers and a slightly longer, pitch black hoodie. Hm maybe he'd been right about me after all because I could definitely see myself stealing one like that.

"Quick! How would you wear this hoodie?" he asked when he noticed me admiring it. The stylist part of my brain answered as I turned to gather the last few garments and accessories even though the rest knew what he was up to.

"As a dress. No belt. Docs. Chrome hearts jewelry. Maybe a camo messenger bag and at least one thing from an indie designer."

"See? I knew you could do it," he said triumphantly then made a disclaimer that he hoped he didn't offend me with what he would say next. That made my ears perk up. "Obviously I'm no expert at this fashion stuff, but I see that you're wearing black nail polish. Is that coming back into style?"

Oh now he was trying to be funny.

"It never left for me," I said matter-of-factly as I twirled my spirit fingers. "It's the last holdover from my very dark, but fun emo adolescence."

"Really? You? I couldn't imagine you like that," he said like I hadn't been dressed in all black every time he'd seen me so far.

"Yep and I've got the pictures to prove it, aside from my questionable hair choices then I don't cringe too much because black has always looked good on me. It's why I stick with it when I'm on the road too. It travels well, it's functional and matches easily."

"Sure, black and every other color, huh?" he asked decidedly skipping over the rest of my spiel and another chunk of my coal lump heart fell from my chest.

I had to make him stop while I still had a chance.

Now gripping the heavy garments for dear life, I turned to him. "Are you planning on hitting on me like this the whole time we're here together or are you just getting it all out of your system now?"

He jolted slightly, taken aback at my directness.

"No, of course not. Why, would you be open to that sort of thing if I was?"

"What sort of thing?"

"Dating. Well not dating. A date. A single date to see how long you can stand to be around me," he rambled and I could tell that I had thrown off his confidence some.

For a split second he was no longer Easton Woods and just another regular nervous guy asking out a girl he liked.

You could've heard a pin drop. My arms were starting to scream from the weight of the clothes, but I didn't care. All I knew was that against my better judgement, I was seriously considering risking it all for a night alone with this impish, spoiled man and his hoodie.

Then a voice in my head made me stop and think of Max. I had promised. I'd said that I would get this done then get back home.

And I would.

I could literally feel my bottom half screaming in rebellion, but I took a deep breath and did the right thing.

"Actually I think it would be best if we didn't complicate things and just kept a professional relationship."

Easton nodded ruefully, "Oh yeah, that would probably be best."

The pang of disappointment in his voice surprised me but not more than what he followed it up with.

"Look, I'm sorry if I stepped over the line or made you uncomfortable, okay? I just...I guess I thought there was something there so I went for it."

"It's fine and you didn't make me feel uncomfortable at all. But if you don't mind stepping out of my way because my arms are about to fall off from all of these clothes."

He smiled. "Cool. I'll be leaving in a few. Did you still want to talk about any other appearances this week?"

"Yeah. Just hold on a sec. Chad is waiting on me to drop these off first."

I did my best to gather my scattered thoughts as I walked away. I was nearly breathless remembering the times that I'd ridden out with Cayenne to the far reaches of fields on a moonlight-soaked night to watch the stars and sleep under the sky, only to return before anybody was up.

Those times had felt like possibility and freedom, so playful, sensual and alluring that it had felt like my whole body and self had come to life. Easton made me think of that, of what was possible yet mysterious and undiscovered.

And maybe I had spoken too soon. After a year in the dumps I deserved to have some fun and a date didn't have to mean forever. I would still be home soon.

I left the returns in Chad's capable hands then went back to Easton's dressing room ready to see if he was still up to hanging out. This time though I heard him on a call so I stopped at the door, not wanting to interrupt his conversation.

"Tell me everything! What did you say and what did she say and then what did you say?" a lively girlish voice questioned.

"Uh I can't really get into everything right now, El, but she said no."

El? As in Eleanor "Elly" Woods? Oh my god. He was talking to his sister about me!

"Really? I thought you said you were in the zone and charming her pants off," she snorted out.

"Uh…guess I was wrong," he replied through a forced chuckle.

"Well are you gonna try again?"

He was silent for a few seconds then replied, "No. She

seems like she just wants to do her job so I'm saving the rest of my charm for a rainy day."

"I get it, but don't let it get you too down. You've still got plenty of other options."

"Don't remind me," he said sarcastically which made her laugh.

"Oh stop it with your 'Every girl wants me, but do they really want *me*, El?' whining," she teased by mocking his deep voice.

"Do I think going after another stylist is a good idea after what you went through with Jade last year? No, but I still think enough time has passed for you to get back out there. The work you've put in for this whole career pivot has been nothing short of amazing, but you know there's more to life than the grind, Easy Peasy."

"Yeah I hear you, Smelly Elly," he said playfully after a sigh then changed the subject.

I stepped back from the cracked door, making sure I still wasn't spotted as I leaned against the corridor wall. I needed a minute to think about what I'd just heard because it wasn't at all what I'd expected. It sounded like the playboy image that he'd been leaning into was just that—an image—since his dating life was actually about as lackluster as mine had been since I'd ended things with Jake.

That one little detail piqued my curiosity and suddenly made me want to know who he really was now so I walked up and knocked on the door, not waiting for permission before I entered.

Startled, Easton said, "Hey El, let me call you right back."

"Tell her you'll call her back tomorrow. Change of plans. We're going out."

"Going where?" his confused brows seemed to ask as he ended the call.

"Does it really matter?" I asked forwardly then laughed when he admitted that it indeed did not.

I took him to my all-time favorite brick oven pizza place since pizza and beer constituted an entire food group for me. Even though it was a weekend night, Easton was able to use some of that rainy day charm on the hostess so she could give us a private spot on the second floor, but sadly, we were already about to have our first fight.

"I don't believe you just ordered a salad. In the face of London's best brick oven pizza, you ordered a salad?"

He shrugged. "My character has naked scenes in my next movie so I've got to watch what I eat 'til we wrap."

"Afraid one little slice will make you lose one of your twenty abs?" I asked teasingly then pretended to count them all.

"I don't have twenty abs and besides I had a piece of chocolate with my lunch so I'm already down to nineteen now."

There it was, that mischievous look again. Oh, I had

made a good choice. This would be a fun night.

"Wait." He raised an eyebrow at me. "Don't tell me you've been checking out my body, Penny?"

"Not on purpose, but it's kind of hard to miss."

"Well now I don't know how I feel about you being in my dressing rooms. As a professional you're supposed to make it your duty not to sexualize me in any way," he said almost convincingly.

"Oh please. You grew up in Hollywood. I think you'll live."

"Actually I grew up in Beverly Hills so it's a little different, but even then my parents were dead set against anybody else raising me and Elly so we pretty much went on location with them all the time. I didn't like it much then, but looking back it helped us miss a lot of stuff that other kids our age got into. How about you?"

"Well I was raised on a farm in Northern Illinois, about an hour outside of Chicago. And yes before you ask, we've got it all, cows, pigs, chickens and lots of corn. But my favorite part has always been getting to ride the horses."

"Whoa. I wasn't expecting that. What made you leave the farm?"

"Well when you live in a town with five thousand people, you're bound to kiss a cousin or two after a while which wasn't really my thing."

"Lucky for me," he said nodding along with a smile. "But I meant how did a farm kid get into styling?" He sounded genuinely interested so I gave him the unabridged version.

"Well my mama was a wardrobe specialist with the Joffrey Ballet and used to be a dancer herself. She tried to teach all her girls about clothes and dance, but I was the only one that absorbed the fashion stuff since we all still have two left feet."

He grinned. "How many sisters do you have?"

"Two. It goes Max, me then Simone even though she likes to act like she's the boss of us sometimes."

"Do they still work on the farm?"

"Simone teaches, but she helps sometimes. Max and I were actually waiting for my parents to retire so we could take over everything together, but I don't know if that will happen anymore. Life challenges and stuff, you know?" I tried to keep my voice as light and steady as possible, hoping that he'd want to change the subject because I didn't like to talk about Max's business too much.

"I hear you. So do you come from a long line of farmers then?"

"No and it's funny because my daddy started out as a biochemist. The only reason he started the corn farm was because of an experiment gone horribly wrong. We always joke that his entire life was one big accident," I said which made his eyes widen before I clarified.

"No I meant because he met my mama by accident too. His boss ended up with an extra ticket to the Joffrey winter gala and gave it to him. She was there and it was instant magic."

"Sounds like how my parents met."

"Yeah except my mama didn't get spirited away to a tropical island."

"Well one thing you can say about the Woods men is that when we want somebody, we don't like to beat around the bush," he said punctuating his sentence with eye contact.

I was about to delve a little deeper into that, but the food arrived and I instantly began stuffing my face with not a bit of shame. And although the pizza was top notch, it really had nothing on the company. Easton was full of interesting stories and surprisingly loved to read so he had great opinions and followed current events closely.

The sexiest thing though was that he listened to me because so many men didn't do that well. Jake had been a complete failure at active listening which had always left me feeling like I was just talking to myself. That was absolutely not the case with Easton.

I was able to share little bits with him, let him see the little pieces of myself I'd hidden since the breakup. Already just being there with him had made the daring side of me resurface. It felt like taking up the reigns in my hands and leading Cayenne out into the night for an adventure. I was opening up to something bigger than myself and after not doing that for a while it felt really good.

Finally as we waited for the check Easton said, "Alright, that was your part of the date. Now I get to give you something."

"Is it that ab that you claim to have lost because I could really use it?" I joked after putting a hand on my full tummy.

He smirked. "No. It's something better. Just let me text somebody to make sure we can get in."

"Ooh now I'm intrigued."

A year ago I would have asked a million questions about where we were going or who would be there but not now. I planned on just following his lead because for now at least I trusted him.

The rideshare drove us around for a while, finally turning into an open scrollwork metal gate that opened to a circular driveway rimmed with cars and trailers. For a minute I wondered if the driver had gotten lost until Easton thanked him and got out. Offering his hand, he helped me up then walked us over to the front door. I felt more fluttering in my stomach than should have been allowed so soon and prayed that he didn't notice my hand when it started to tremble a little bit in his.

We seemed to be at one of those old, stately British homes where you would expect to see some distressed damsel running around in a Jane Austen era empire-waist white gown and cloak. I'd never had the time to visit an old English manor house before, but it felt like stepping into a storybook just like I'd imagined.

"Where are we?"

"Twombly house, one of the movie locations. It's a gorgeous old place that's a museum now, but we're using it as my character's family home."

"Are they still shooting this late?"

"Just a few people doing prep and some night shots in a far garden out back. I think they just wrapped up most of it, but we probably won't run into anybody since they're mostly in the production trailers right now." He walked up the steps to a large black door then turned the doorknob. "Perfect. Door's open like my friend said. Let's go."

We entered a dimly lit foyer decorated with an interesting mix of baroque antiques and 1930s style art. Easton kept going through room after room, not rushing, but not really giving me much time to stop and take in the scenery.

"Sorry I'm not giving you a really good tour," he offered like he had read my mind. "It's getting late so I don't want to keep you out too long, but if you want I can bring you back so you can see the set fully dressed up."

"Okay, but where are we headed now?" For some reason, we were whispering like we were on some super secret mission or something.

"You'll know it when you see it.

He went down a hallway, made some more turns then reached a set of French doors. Opening one side, he ushered me inside then quickly closed it after us.

I still couldn't see where we were, but I could smell dirt and hear the faintest rustling of leaves. Through the glass windows overhead I saw the bright light of the moon shining through a smattering of stars and realized that we were in a very large solarium chock full of plants.

"Is there any light in here?" I asked curious to see what was around us.

Easton turned on his phone flashlight then walked over to the wall. After a moment, I heard him say, "Got it."

I nearly gasped as the room filled with small beacons of white. There were string lights all through the plants, draped on trees, twinkling like Christmas. It was just enough light to see the deep green of the leaves as they concealed a plant-covered, intimate little seating area just for two near the very back of the room.

"Easton, this is...wow." I wandered around just taking it all in. "I've never seen anything as pretty as this."

"It's great, isn't it? Apparently the matriarch of the family was a huge botany fanatic and she asked visitors to bring clippings instead of other presents when they'd stay."

"They obviously listened. It's incredible."

Easton stripped off his coat then came up behind me, his hands softly cupping my shoulders.

"It's warm in here. Want to take your coat off?"

"Sure," I sighed, enjoying the feel of his arm and leg pressed against mine after he'd gotten us settled on the bench.

It was nonsexual contact, but it was late, I'd had plenty of beer to relax and I was suddenly the horniest I'd been in years. The time was ripe for me to make some very bad decisions.

I wanted nothing more than to just throw him down right then and there, but I wasn't exactly in the mood to explain impromptu sexcapades to any of his hapless coworkers who might discover us, but...it was late and they were all engrossed in their work. No. No. No. I was making excuses.

Down, girl, down.

"In the movie, what happens in this room?" I asked trying to distract myself by looking at all the lights and plants around us.

"Well," he began before using a finger to direct my face back over to his to look in his eyes while he spoke. "My character, a very lustful but honorable man named Daniel professes his undying love for a very sweet but headstrong lady the night before he leaves for war."

"What do you say to her?"

"A bunch of very earnest stuff about how she's his soulmate and beacon of light and that he'll think about her even as the final bullet pierces his body."

"How romantic. Yes, think of her as a bullet shoots you dead."

He chuckled. "It was a different time. We couldn't have even gone out on this date without a chaperone back then, but look how far we've come as a society now," he said sarcastically as he leaned in closer to me so that our noses touched.

I'd thought that he might kiss me and was disappointed when he didn't, but just like I'd done to kick off the date I decided to take matters into my own hands.

"I know right. They definitely would've frowned at all the premarital sex we're about to have in here soon."

There, I said it. No turning back now.

From that point forward I deemed words to be a useless form of communication because not only did nothing else need to be said, not that it could have with our mouths locked together like magnets, but we both seemed to prefer the way our bodies had started to speak to one another.

My fingers eventually left his beautiful face and found the ripples of his stomach and traveled around to his tight sides. I pulled myself against him, taking in the slight musk of his body from a long day of work mixed with the clean freshness of his grooming products. His five o'clock shadow rubbed my face slightly as he nuzzled my ears and tasted the side of my neck.

I bit back a moan as he found my sweet spot and nipped it ever so slightly. That little sound caused him to groan back in response and I just about turned into a fire pit in his arms.

It wasn't clear whether he had pulled me into his lap or if I'd planted myself there. What I did know, however, was that my panties were getting completely soaked and that I could now feel that he was packing something quite intimidating in his pants. I also realized that I had no qualms about bringing those body parts together right on this bench and treating Easton like Cayenne and riding him right past nighttime into sunrise.

"We really need to stop," he suddenly said while still licking and kissing another spot on my neck. "Somebody's gonna walk in and see us."

I backed up slightly, but before I could let my sense of propriety shut me up, I leaned up and ran the tip of my tongue along Easton's jawline. Just the thought of doing that over more real estate drove me nuts and killed any little embers of guilt or modesty I might have had.

I swore I felt his erection grow even more under those snug jeans of his as he took in my words. "You're full of surprises tonight."

"I would rather be full of you," I told him honestly as I ran my fingers under the hemline of his shirt to feel the soft heat of his skin.

Easton's quiet groan let me know that he wouldn't need any more convincing. After taking a quick look around, he put me back on the bench then walked over to the lights to at least give the illusion of privacy. A moment of work then we were plunged back into darkness and faint traces of shadowy moonlight. What I could still make out of his quite sizable bulge through his jeans let me know that he was just as turned on as I was in the moment.

As my nerves melted away my hands started to wander and I eventually pulled off his hoodie. I had no intentions of stealing it though so he could have it back when I was done with him. He in turn ran his hand down my legs then unzipped my boots one at a time, chucking them on the floor.

For once in my life I found that I'd worn the perfect top for sexy time: a silk blouse with a deep V neck. Easton trailed a finger from the base of my neck, all the way down to the one snap I'd sewn in to make it work appropriate. I sighed then wriggled as his tongue followed the finger, creating a warm path down to my cleavage. His fingers popped the snap and my bra-caged girls were suddenly front and center for his delectation.

"What I want to do to you, Penny," he whispered out almost like he was in pain, "there's just not enough time in the day."

I gasped as his lips discovered my neck again and teased my nipples with his fingers. He'd pushed down one side of my blouse and was now sucking on me through the lace of my bra. My clit went from pleasantly fiery to combustion hot in an instant as his teeth played with my flesh, the moist heat and roughened textile combining to drive me nuts. My back arched, pushing me into his mouth even more.

I nearly tore off his t-shirt and tossed it away, craving the skin on skin contact that I'd been thinking about since we were alone in his dressing room. He pulled my shirt off right after and the sound that came out of me when his flesh touched mine sounded like it came from a starving animal, but I couldn't be bothered to care.

His hands reached around to unsnap my bra as my fingers fumbled with the waistband of his jeans. He cupped my breast in one hand then plied the nipple with his tongue as he lazily toyed with the other, teasing me to hell and back. All the while I was doing my best to stifle the noises that wanted to burst from me, but it was a struggle.

While still having his idea of fun with my girls, he dragged me to the very edge of the bench. I could feel cool air caressing my nether regions as he pushed my skirt up to my waist then worked himself between my legs. Lifting my knee up, he nibbled and licked all the way down to the good stuff.. No hesitation, no taking my panties off, just straight sliding them over to get to the goods.

"Keep quiet," he instructed softly as he started to fool around with my clit. "You don't want anybody to know what I'm about to do to your pussy, right?"

"I...oh, my god..." Needless to say, he didn't wait for an answer to start feasting.

It had been way too long since anybody had taken care of business down there, but it took no time before I was reminded just how sensitive I was. My hips took on a life of their own and I couldn't help but reach up and pinch my nipples as he ate, drank and slurped at me with wild abandon. My head was twisting back and forth as I bit my lip, desperate to not let one sound out.

Because Easton was an overachiever and he could see that I was barely holding it together, he hooked my right knee over his shoulder and gave himself even better access to me. He filled me with a long, adept finger as he pressed down on the top of my mound, adding pressure and stimulating me to my limits.

"Easton, please stop!" I begged as I ground my hips on his hand in desperation and gave more harsh pinches to my nipples, enjoying the bolt of sensation that shot down to my clit.

"No," he told me in defiance as he added another finger and sipped from my body again. "I want some more."

I whimpered at his words as his tongue applied pressure and his hooked fingers threw me into the deepest, most intense orgasm that my body could process. Sensing my sudden loss of composure, he used his free hand to cover my mouth as I let out the long, guttural battle cry that had been sitting in my chest for the last few minutes.

When I came to again I heard a tearing sound, smelled the faint scent of a fresh condom then felt him rub the hard, round head of his penis up and down along my swollen lower lips. Lowering himself on top of me, he let his mouth rest against mine for a lazy minute and let me taste myself on his breath.

"You ready for me?"

"Do it," I dared him, still weak but still hungry for him too.

Easton worked himself in inch by inch, ignoring all

roadblocks and demanding space inside of me. That shadowy pant print was living up to its promise and I groaned as my body was forced to stretch around him.

"Fuck Penny, you're a tight fit," he moaned out as he fully seated himself then went still. Well some of him went still because he never stopped pulsing and making himself at home in me.

Feeling impatient, I moved my hips and swiveled around his length, determined to make him as crazy as he had made me. We started to move together, every motion slow and drawn out, each feeling intense enough to make my toes curl and teeth clench. I had never been one to scratch a guy's back, but I let my black claws dig into his skin just enough to count to goad him into picking up the pace.

We found the perfect inviting groove in no time, but the sound of approaching footsteps caused us both to tense up and bring it to a halt.

"Is that your friend?" I mouthed to him, but he shook his head no and stayed perfectly still.

Whoever it was they were hanging out in the doorway, not really coming or going. The front of the solarium was pretty dark, so it was possible that they didn't see our coats piled up, but then again, our coats were black so they could easily pass as a pile of random fabric. There was practically no way to know we were there.

My back started to ache slightly from the lack of movement so I adjusted slightly. Easton's eyes almost rolled back into his head as I corkscrewed around him.

He shot me a pleased but disapproving look and I shot him one back.

Then came the unmistakable sound of the phone ringing.

"Hello? Hey, Pete. Just wanted to give you the rundown of that change to the set for the garden scene. Got a minute?"

Suddenly, Easton glided himself in to the hilt then drew back. Then did it again. And again. Never hard enough to create a slapping sound or any other noise, but decisive enough to make me realize that he was no longer deterred by our unwitting audience. In fact he seemed turned on by it.

It was so wrong. That was why I stayed perfectly still and spread, taking him in each time, being a good girl and not uttering a peep. I'd never had adventurous sex or risked getting caught, but I felt like I'd taken a shot of aphrodisiac straight to my best parts.

Sweat poured off Easton and dripped off onto me, our scents mixing with the woodsy ones around us as I abandoned all hope of any control. How could something as mundane as a phone call be happening close by when I was burning alive?

Easton sped up, a silent force on top of me, purposefully

applying force on my clit as he thrust and thrust into me. I'd never felt my orgasm hit as hard as it did then. Not with Jake and definitely not with anybody else before Easton.

As I clenched around him his hand gripped my hair and he kissed me hard, swallowing my sobs as I convulsed underneath and all around him. A moment later he followed, his low rumbling groan vibrating throughout me as he emptied himself into our layer of protection, but an electrifying part of him had still somehow made its way into me.

The door eventually clicked shut in the distance and we both were able to relax into a floppy mass of sweaty euphoria.

Easton kissed my head then gently released my leg, but all I could do was lie there helpless and still open but satisfied beyond belief.

"You still with me, gorgeous?" he asked almost smugly, but he had done such a good job that it bothered me none.

I barely had enough energy to reply but mustered up enough for a quick lie, "Yeah. Yep, I'd say so," before ultimately admitting that I needed a second to recover.

His cocky grin hovered over me but disappeared when he brought himself back down to sweetly kiss my lips.

"Hurry up and catch your breath. Now that I know you like to ride horses, I've got something else in mind."

And that's exactly what I was afraid of.

UPGRADE YOU

The next two and a half weeks were sheer bliss. Somehow, Easton and I dated yet no one figured out our little secret.

It was really something else. We sat together at fashion shows, did our shoots and attended the pressers. You would've never known we were together unless you really knew what to look for, but that was by design.

When I was a kid I remember trying to hide surprises and happy secrets from my family and failing miserably because I would never be able to contain my joy. I'd always be the last one to find out about surprise parties because I was guaranteed to spill the beans and ruin everything. Now though since my professional reputation relied on us keeping things under wraps, I kept my damned mouth shut even when it was a near impossibility.

All day I'd been fantasizing about dinner the night before. Easton had taken me to a really intimate little spot then back to the house he was renting for drinks. Of course drinks had turned into me bent over the arm of the couch and moaning my head off while he had his way with me, but that was just an added perk to our time together. Yeah the sex was nice, but I had gotten to know Easton much more than I'd intended to. He was more than just my secret London lover now. He'd turned into a sort of friend too.

That was why even though the movie had re-wrapped a few days ago he and I were was already thinking of awards season. I had ideas for some great red carpet looks and my efforts had paid off in the best way: Easton's image was slowly but surely taking a decisive turn from comedic pretty boy to possible dramatic powerhouse.

He had signed onto a new movie that would start shooting in a few weeks and he'd already decided that along with everything else about me that he was highly pleased with my styling too. We were already making plans of all kinds for the weeks and months ahead and Mikel was very happy to hear that I no longer needed convincing to keep on trucking.

When I spoke to Simone that afternoon, I would break the news that I wouldn't be home as quickly as I'd thought but that we'd still definitely have more than enough cash to reach our goals for the retreat center. I'd even have enough to keep me afloat while I established some other income streams and projects.

"Penny!" Denise called out much louder than necessary to get my head out of the clouds since it had been up there a lot lately. "Teegan Ravin is on the phone for you."

"Oh, great," I muttered before putting in my earbuds then speaking in the most bland, civil tone I could muster. "This is Penny Pope."

"Hello, Penny. Teegan Ravin here. How are you?"

My eyes involuntarily rolled themselves because this viper didn't give a damn about how I was doing.

"Just wrapping up loose ends here before I start my awards season projects. Did you need help with another client?"

"Not at the moment. I just wanted to touch base with you and say that everything turned out looking great and we're getting exactly the sort of outcomes that we wanted with Easton. I just told Mikel that I'd be adding a bonus because you deserve it."

"Well thank you." I looked at the phone like it was possessed. This was not the same Teegan that I had verbally confronted then put in her place last year. "I do still have some comped garments from a few designers that I want to use for future events. Easton's pics really exposed him to some great opportunities with some strong designers and it would be good to cultivate those relationships."

"I agree. I'll pass that on to Ana Beatriz when I talk to her next. She'll definitely want to work on that going into awards season, you know? And the historical drama just opens all sorts of doors creatively."

Hold up, what?!

"Ana Beatriz Cardoza, the stylist?"

"Oh, yes. We've hired her to work with Easton from here forward. I'd always intended on her taking over after the film anyway. Image transitions aren't her strong suit and Mikel asked for a favor since you'd been out of work for so long."

It was pretty hard to speak around a lump of disappointment so huge that it threatened to choke you. For a minute I panicked, thinking that she must have known about me and Easton. Maybe she wanted to separate us because we'd looked too intimate? I didn't know. What

I did know was that I'd die before I let her upset me or ruin my composure in any way.

"Well it was a pleasure transforming Easton and if there's anything I can do to help Ana Beatriz, let me know and I'll have Denise write up notes," I said trying to sound unbothered when I was far from it.

When I hung up, I told Denise I was going to take a little break from the hotel's conference space we'd been working out of then went up to my room.

It was all I could do to not start crying. Why should I have been upset though? Simone would be happy to have me home earlier and I could finally spend more time with Max. My end goal had always been to be back home as soon as possible anyway, not traipsing around the world and mixing with people who had the personality of a piece of glammed-up plywood. If only somebody else hadn't brought a new level of excitement to that space in his own special, secret way.

Simone picked up the phone on the second ring and I wasted no time dramatically bursting into tears and blowing my cover.

"Honey, what happened? Did Easton Woods do something to you?!"

"No! Oh, god, no. Simone. I've very *willingly* been with him these last few weeks. We hang out all the time and he's so sweet and he loves his family so much and and--"

"Oh god, you love him, don't you?!" she teasingly squealed as I flopped back on the bed and stared at the ceiling.

"No! Of course not!" I denied even though I had been feeling something way past like lately.

"Yes you do! Hold on. I'm gonna vomit then go tell, Ma."

"No please don't. This wasn't supposed to happen. I had a plan!"

"And that's exactly why it happened, because you had a big ol' plan! I told you about that, didn't I?" She continued to tease me before the reason why I'd called suddenly hit her in the face. "Oh so now that you're in love with the pretty boy, you don't want to come home anymore, right?"

"No. My work here is done and Teegan gave my damn job away to Ana Beatriz Cardoza so there's not much I can do at this point anyway."

"Well maybe it's for the best that you come home and don't get in any deeper. He's a big star and he doesn't have the best track record with women so let's be real here. You don't want another Jake situation and Max really misses you too."

Just hearing her name made me close my eyes then focus for a moment.

"Right. You're right. Thanks for listening to my little freak out. Listen, I need to get going. I have lunch with you-know-who in forty minutes."

"Well, have fun while you can. Just know that it's gonna come to an end so don't make it into more than what it is."

...

Easton always left the door open for me so I walked right in after arriving at his place. I immediately wondered when he'd decided to become a florist because from the foyer all the way to the dining room it looked and smelled like a wedding waiting to happen or maybe a funeral. The way my life had been going that day it would definitely be the funeral.

I saw roses, tulips and many other flowers that I thought were pretty and had seen before but just didn't remember their names. Since I had a black thumb it seemed a little cruel to memorize the names of all the probable murder victims so I'd never really bothered to learn.

Meanwhile the table was already set and full of food: a beautiful green salad, cold shrimp, oysters, lobster, fresh bread, chilled white wine and cheese. I'd told Easton about a terrific meal I'd had once with some of these things and it was adorable that he'd tried to recreate it for me.

He walked into the room with a bucket of ice looking devastatingly handsome as usual in a soft blue button-down shirt and a pair of drawstring pants that I recognized from the last shoot I'd done with him. I loved them on him so much that he'd purchased a couple pairs right after.

"Hey you're here! Surprise!" he said before coming over to give me a loud, smacking kiss on the lips. "What do you think?"

Because I had no chill whatsoever, I immediately started bawling again. And not a gentle, ladylike cry either. Oh, no. It was a gross, deep ugly cry. Easton looked startled and a little bit alarmed.

"What is it? Are the flowers too much? I can throw them off the balcony if you want," he joked but probably would have done it if I'd asked. Instead I shook my head then snorted up a whole bunch of snot.

"No, no! The flowers are perfect. Everything is perfect! It's not that."

"Then what is it? This isn't like you. Did something happen?"

I took a deep breath to calm down a little bit because I was a split second away from grabbing a fork off the table and putting myself out of my misery. I needed something, anything, to quell the feeling of dread that had been sitting in my body for the last hour or so.

"Teegan fired me today. Or no, let me change that. She hired a new stylist for you and I'll probably be flying out soon. That's what's wrong." I wiped my nose with the back of my hand. "And it just hit me how much I've loved these last few weeks and it kills me that it's over already."

He looked at me for a second before speaking then handed me a few paper towels.

"Uh, here. So you don't have to, you know, use your..." he added as he imitated me wiping with my hand.

"Oh, right." I blew my nose even harder then tried to wipe away my tears. "Thank you. You're so sweet and I just went all unhinged on your plans and ruined everything. I'm sorry."

Always a cuddle monster who loved having me sit on his lap, Easton settled into his big, wide recliner then put his arms around me tightly.

"I had no idea that Teegan had done that, but it was a stupid move on her part and I'll fix it," he promised before softly kissing the top of my head.

"No, no. It's probably useless at this point. I'm sure she booked Ana Beatriz a while ago and it's not like I don't have things to do back in Spring Grove anyway."

"Yeah, but I'm not letting you do that. Teegan works for me and I'll just pay this woman to go away so don't worry about any of this."

"Do you hear yourself right now? This is your career, your baby and you've worked hard to get these opportunities. I hate to admit it, but Ana Beatriz really is the best and she has great connections."

"I don't care. I think you're the best and the only connection I care about right now is ours. What the hell good is it if I don't have you with me telling me what to buy and challenging my policy of hoodie supremacy?" he joked before his eyes synced with mine again then went serious. "Penny, if you're not here anymore then this all becomes just...work."

This was too much emotional upheaval. My therapist was going to have a field day with our next video appointment.

Finally remembering my conversation with Simone, I sat up and looked Easton straight in the eye.

"I don't think this is a good idea anymore."

"What's not a good idea?" he asked even though it was quite

obvious, but he was going to make me say the words.

The answer was all of it. I hadn't put very much thought into it before then because I'd figured we would just be a fling, but if we were to start dating seriously then I suppose that it might sort of bother me that I would be the second stylist that he'd hired then humped. And sure being around him so much had shown me that he was nothing like Jake, but being with a famous man let alone one as beautiful as Easton would always come with a headache.

Jake's fame hadn't been that big of a deal at first either, but our nice, sweet early relationship had turned into a tense, embarrassing and anxiety-filled ordeal for me by the end. And how could it not when one person made their living in front of cameras and the other person had developed an entire career out of the limelight?

"It's just that I like being able to go to the store or out shopping with friends without people taking pictures of me. Styling can be, but it isn't exactly a high visibility, high fame type of job, you know? But you... you're about to become even bigger than you already are. Are you sure you want to start dating right now?"

I knew he'd been listening to me because he always did, but he barely let me finish speaking before coming back with something so sweet and genuine that it felt like it could have been ripped from one of his movies.

"Penny, I know you still haven't seen any of my movies yet, but right now I need you to trust me when I tell you that I'm a great actor, okay? And that doesn't just mean that I'm good at memorizing my lines or crying on cue. It means that I can recognize when other people are acting too and I love that since the second I met you, you haven't pretended to be anything other than who you are down to the color of your nails."

"Easton--"

"No. You, farmer girl, are one of the good ones and I'm going to show you a very good time for as long as you'll let me. Understood?" he said putting his foot down as he reached out for me to lie back into him.

It was impossible to resist the impulse to snuggle into them so I didn't even try. I was sure that I didn't quite love him yet, but I sure did love those arms around me. I'd always been a very sensual type of girl and it had been a long while since I'd been around a man like this. As his arms tightened around me, the realization that the feeling really was mutual washed over me and brought a wave of satisfaction. In that moment I decided to temporarily put Max and the rest of my worries behind me because bliss was mine.

"Oh and you actually do have one more job to finish," he said to my surprise after cuddling for a while.

Frowning, I thought back to the schedule. Had Denise forgotten to tell me something? "What did I miss?"

"There's a little wrap party in Vegas. Turns out that there's a music festival happening this weekend so a bunch of the crew are gonna fly over and unwind for a couple days."

"But you don't need me for that. You've been around me long enough to throw something decent together without my help," I complimented as I ran my hands down his current ensemble.

"I don't know. If you don't come then I might be forced to find a suit jacket to bring back— what did you call it—hoodie-tux? I might need to trademark that," he said then picked up his phone like he was taking a note before I playfully slapped him on the chest.

"Over my dead body, which might still happen because I'm still feeling pretty miserable right now. I was just eyeing the forks and thinking very bad things."

"Not the forks!"

"Yes, the forks, but I guess I'd better not do that if I'm gonna save you from embarrassing yourself in Vegas."

"So you'll come with me?"

I thought it over quickly. It would be one last weekend with him before we'd more than likely part ways forever or try to do some ridiculous long distance thing that would inevitably peter out so why not? What did I have to lose?

Plus I was a stylist, not a superstar and I'd taken care to keep a low profile for most of my career especially for the last year so everything would be fine.

"I'll go, but who's gonna pay me for my styling services?" I asked as I tapped his pockets. "I'm a businesswoman and my rates are not cheap. I need answers and a contract ASAP, Woods."

He gazed at me in that sinful way that I knew meant he wanted to enjoy a different type of spread than what he'd prepared for me on the table.

"I've got your contract right here, Penny," he began as he adjusted me on his lap so that he could look down at it, "and would you look at that? Your name is already on it."

...

True to his word Easton took care of me. Three days later as I ate a sensible goodbye breakfast with Denise, I got a text from him to be downstairs a quarter before noon with all of my luggage. I'd boxed up most of my things and shipped them back to the states, but kept some of the items that I figured I'd want in Vegas.

Like a gentleman he'd offered to come help me with everything, but I declined because I had Denise and she still didn't suspect a thing between us which was good. I was amazed that I'd been able to keep our dating situation under wraps for the entire trip, but I suppose that she was so busy sneaking around with Amal that she didn't have time to notice us.

The hotel phone rang just as I was closing my last suitcase.

"Hello, Ms. Pope. Your driver has arrived downstairs. Would you like the porter to come get your things?"

Ah Easton. Coming through with the VIP treatment.

"Yes, that would be fine. Thanks."

"Good morning, gorgeous!" He gave me a kiss and put his arm around me as we pulled away from the hotel. "Ready for Vegas? I brought you coffee." He motioned towards the two cups in the drink holder.

"Thanks handsome. I think I'm ready, but a better question is 'Is Vegas ready for us?'"

He laughed. "I guess we'll find out. I've been looking forward to this weekend for the past few days. The PR people for the festival really laid out the red carpet for everybody."

"How many people are going?"

He stopped and thought for a second. "At least fifty."

"Hm. Nice sized crowd. What time did you book our plane tickets for?"

"Plane tickets?" he asked like I had suddenly spoken a foreign language.

"Yeah the things that let you on the plane so you don't have to ride on the wing. A plane ticket."

"Yeah you don't need those on a private jet," he replied, sipping on the cup of coffee. "And we take off at two."

Well that was unexpected. I didn't think he was being paid quite that well just yet.

"You have a jet?"

"No, it belongs to my family. It's one of the few wasteful things my parents have always indulged in for convenience, but otherwise we keep it pretty simple."

"Not sure I believe you after the surprise jet."

"No really. A lot of my parents' friends have staff and these huge homes, with more cars than they'll ever drive in their lifetime. We never did that. My mom and dad didn't want us growing up to be Beverly Hills nightmare children with a huge sense of entitlement and no grounding whatsoever."

I watched the pedestrians and buildings as we passed, wishing I'd had more time to enjoy all the fun stuff that London had to offer. A fleeting thought popped up that said we might visit again some day just for pleasure, but I shooed it away to the back of my mind.

"That sounds sensible. If I ever have kids, that's how I want them raised."

He paused. "So you do want kids someday too?"

"Yeah I love them. Once I get my business off the ground in Spring Grove, I can start thinking about the future. It seems pretty far off right now though, you know?"

Something I said made Easton turn a bit serious. "Back in Spring Grove? That's where you're headed?"

I kept my eyes on the road in front of me as I nodded because I didn't want to see any disappointment in his eyes.

"Yeah. Me and my sisters are starting a retreat and recovery center on the plot of land right next to my parents' farm. We just have to finish up some renovations then we're going to open in the fall. We're calling it the Maxine Pope center."

"After your one sister? Why not all three of you?"

When I didn't answer right away he looked over to make sure

that I was okay. And I was. It was just I'd never told anybody about Max before so this was a first and I was taken aback at how much I was letting him in.

"About a year ago Max found out that her husband had been cheating on her and when she threatened to leave, he didn't take it so well. He tried to kill her and himself, but we got our miracle and she somehow survived a bullet to the chest with mostly just emotional damage. It went clean through her and out the other side."

"Wow, that's insane!" he exclaimed. It was a good thing we were stopped at a traffic light because all of his attention immediately went to me. "Is she okay now?" he asked sounding genuinely concerned and it warmed my heart since he didn't know anything about her except that I loved her.

"No," I said honestly. "But she's getting better every day and I know that opening the center will be another big step in the right direction."

Before pressing down on the gas again he pressed his lips into my hand then said, "I'm proud of you for what you're doing for her. You're an even better person than I already knew you were."

With no further words I snuggled into his shoulder and enjoyed the rest of the car ride, finally feeling like I was in the right place with the right man at the right time.

I didn't know why I had ever thought that Vegas was going to be a relaxing time. The Venn diagram between fashion stylists and film people wasn't that large and I definitely hadn't known what I was signing up for when I'd agreed to come because those people partied hard! It turned out that the director, producer, and a couple of the leads had chipped in for a wild weekend in sin city, not a dignified little kaffeeklatsch like I had assumed would happen.

Easton and I reached our room, took a nap and were back out a few hours later for a trip to the shops with a bunch of people. The crowd included some wardrobe techs, some riggers and prop crew and a couple of other actors. Nobody made a big deal about it, but apparently the cat was out of the bag once we met up and Easton made no qualms about grabbing onto my hand.

"Oh, look," he said as we wandered past one shop, "Isn't that the same brand you got that green trench coat from?"

"Yeah, good catch. I'm impressed that you remembered."

He nodded. "Actually, I wouldn't mind going in there and buying one. It looked really good. What do you think?"

"I think that's a great idea. Is this a new Easton I'm seeing?"

Robbie, one of the crew members and a friend of his, clapped him on the back. "Well, Easton's gotta grow up sometime. He's making big moves these days. Right, man?"

"Exactly," Easton replied, looking at me for some reason. "Sometimes a man has to step up and make some changes. Hey Rob, we'll meet you guys downstairs for lunch in a little while, maybe around two?" he said before Robbie and the others wandered off to do their thing.

With us then left to our own devices the real fun started. Easton joked around with salespeople and took pictures with a couple of fans who approached him, but best of all he let me pick out more clothes for him. This time, however, it felt more intimate. He wasn't dressing for an audience of millions. It felt like he was picking for an audience of one. Moi.

I pulled a cashmere hoodie sweater off the rack at one store. "I guess I can let you get one of these for old time's sake."

"Miss Pope, are you feeling okay?" he asked sarcastically as he placed a hand on my forehead. "Because you seem to be suggesting a garment, albeit a fancy one, but still a hooded garment nonetheless."

My cheeks were burning from smiling so much. Why was he so embarrassing and cute at the same time? It hadn't occurred to me until that very second, but I realized then that everything was going to turn out alright. I didn't have all the answers yet, but I was going to enjoy life and make the best of things until they came to me.

After sending the bags back to the hotel with a messenger service, we joined everybody for lunch at a local place near the strip famous for their super-long happy hours. When the first round came around Easton and I drank up because who was going to turn down free booze?

But then there was another. And another.

By the time "lunch" was over at five, Easton and I were happily on our way to being drunk fools.

"Hey, let's go back to the room and get ready. I forgot that Amal got us tickets to that cirque show and he said to get there at seven."

"What, the adult one with the naked people?"

He nodded. "Then we're headed to the first night of the festival at the Cosmo. Don't wear heels for that."

"Bullshit," I slurred a little, waving him off. "I can dance in heels."

"I meant, don't wear heels because otherwise I'm going to end up doing something indecent if I see you in them."

I smirked then slowly licked my lips in his face.

"That sounds like a personal problem to me, Big Easy."

He grinned then raised an eyebrow at me calling him by his tabloid nickname for the first time.

"It's gonna turn into *your* personal problem when I'm inside you against a wall in the dark somewhere," he warned before nudging me in the direction of the exit.

The man had raised more than a good by the time we made it back to the room so as a public service, I took some time out to take care of him before he got us arrested for public indecency.

And yes, I still wore my heels.

But ultimately our pregame romp proved to be a waste of time though because by the time we got to the Cosmo for the festival, I was hot and bothered again. The cirque show had been incredible, but it got us just as turned on as we'd been after lunch. Actually after watching all those beautiful, talented people with practically no clothing doing superhuman feats for more than two hours, Easton and I were completely on the edge of our control.

As we entered the club from the back, the booming house music, flashing lights and high energy of the festival ratcheted up my excitement. The two of us settled into a booth with our party and took in the scenery.

I hadn't even noticed that the bottle girl had set up a table service of chilled champagne, several bottles of hard liquor, and a bunch of mixers. Checking out the assortment, I decided that I was feeling basic and got a vodka cranberry.

Once I had my drink in hand, Easton put his drink up and took my hand in his. "Hey. Cheers to things working out the way you least expect sometimes."

"That's for sure. Cheers back."

He took a sip of his scotch and landed the softest of kisses on my inner wrist, making me shift in my seat a little. It took so very little for him to flip my switch from classy to wanton, but he seemed to have more important things on his mind as he leaned over to speak directly in my ear.

"Listen, I know you're heading back home soon."

"Yeah I have another job lined up, but my agent is still working everything out."

"Right and that's really great, but I have to be honest here." I braced myself as I took a big gulp of my drink. "I don't want you to go."

I looked at him and smiled. "I don't want to go, either, but--"

"Guys!" Perry Dunwell, the director of the movie, plopped down two full shot glasses in front of us. We hadn't even noticed that everybody had gathered in the general vicinity and was holding their own shots. "Get up. We're toasting the movie and it's time to get hammered."

Easton sighed in resignation and cocked up that eyebrow of his. "We'll talk later."

Well, one shot led to two more shots. These movie people loved to talk, my god. Everybody had a speech. Even Easton had something to say. After hearing about so many divas and method acting horror shows over the years, it was stunning to see how well everybody got along.

That didn't happen in fashion a lot. Maybe I was in the wrong line of work, but it was refreshing to see. And of course Easton was there with his charming self, working the crowd, making sure no one was left out or alone.

God, I loved that man.

My drink was resting on my lips when that little thought flitted across my brain. It was true though and I'd be lying if I tried to think differently. I'd fallen completely head over heels for this endearing, earnest, permanently horny pretty boy from 90210.

But Simone had been right. There was no room for this kind of foolishness at this point of my life. I had things to do, commitments to keep. Plus, the logistics would be a nightmare.

I poured another drink and decided to do the mature thing: dance hard and stay drunk in order to deny my emotional chaos, like any other grown woman running away from her problems.

However, it wasn't long before he found his way back over to me. I turned to him and planted a sloppy kiss on his neck as he danced slowly against the beat of the music. He smelled so good I could've stayed in his arms forever.

"Having a good time?"

"The best time, actually."

He looked down at me, a little bit solemn and wistful. "Penny, I think I'm in love with you."

I wasn't sure I'd heard right, what with all the loud music and noise around me. "Did you just say what I think you just said?"

"Let me say it another way. I fucking love you, Penny Pope!" he yelled again near my ear and a few people near us stopped dancing to awe at us.

Everything seemed to go still around me and within me as his words sank in. He loved me.

Looking at him, it felt only natural to say, "And I love you too so, so much. You don't even know."

The amount of joy that came over Easton's face in that moment was unlike anything I'd ever seen before. The realization that I could give that to him made me start to tear up and I held onto him for dear life.

"You're the best thing to happen to me. I can't let you go. You've got to understand that."

"I swear I do. You've got me crying in the club, Easton. Is this really necessary?"

He cupped my face in both hands and kissed me and I melted into his arms, too tipsy to really give a care about who saw what now.

"I don't believe I'm about to say this." He paused. "Let's get married. Tonight."

"Tonight?!" I repeated but more incredulously.

"Tonight! Say yes. Say you'll be my lucky Penny forever," he said so sweet and sincerely that it didn't even matter that he was too drunk to get down on one knee like he'd attempted to do.

And in my euphoric and equally drunken haze, this sounded like the best idea ever. Easton was my new best friend and my partner in crime and he'd made the former emo always dressed in black girl ready to wear white for a change.

"Yes!"

"Yes?!" he asked now being the one who needed confirmation.

"Yes! I'll marry you!"

His fingers were instantly tangled in my hair and a harder, more fervent kiss was planted on my lips this time.

"You won't regret this. I'm going to make you so happy, I promise."

I swore my feelings were spilling from my soul straight to his because he was saying everything that I'd been thinking. And if the past few weeks were any indication, I knew that Easton would make a great husband and take excellent care of me and my heart because besides my dad he was probably the best man I knew. I couldn't say for sure what the future would bring, but I knew that this felt right so we would just have to deal with it when we got there.

THE GLAMOROUS LIFE

I dreamed a bizarre and unsettling dream about people tickling me everywhere I went despite me screaming and begging them not to. It was so strange that even after I woke up alone in bed I swore that I was still being tickled. It turned out to have just been my phone vibrating underneath me the whole time but worse still, my head vibrated along with it and I felt like I'd been hit by a truck. Bleary eyed, I grabbed the phone and saw that my missed call and text count was through the roof.

The most recent message was from Clarence.

I knew he liked you the moment he laid eyes on you. Be a doll and let me throw a post wedding brunch next time you're in the city.

I was still confused and disoriented until I read it a second time and everything suddenly came rushing back to me at once.

Jesus, Mary and Joseph! I had gotten married!

I sat up quickly and instantly regretted it as the room pitched and swayed. Last night hadn't resulted in a sleep-it-off type of drunk. This was an 'I'm still a little drunk the next day' type of drunk. I was still for a second then looked at the nightstand hoping for something to drink to cure my cottonmouth, but instead there was just a large manila envelope marked Saints and Sinners wedding chapel.

The contents included an 8x10 picture that I would soon be burning, a license, a receipt for something called a BAGG kit and two silver rings. And last but certainly not least, there was a marriage certificate signed by yours truly and Earl Woods Jr.

I held up my left hand in shock. Hello, silver ring on the ring finger.

Groaning hard, I fell back on the bed. What the hell had I done? This was insanity. I'd actually gone and married Easton Woods in a Vegas wedding chapel looking like a low-budget Chaka Khan. My parents would kill me and I didn't even want to think of what my sisters would do. Plus worst of all, the man's name was literally Earl so the joke about the TV show practically wrote itself!

Earl Easton obviously hadn't been in bed with me when I'd first woken up, but when I finally heard his voice I was surprised to hear it coming from outside on the balcony through the cracked sliding door. He was pacing and having a heated conversation with somebody so he didn't see me when I scurried by to get to the bathroom.

Hurriedly plopping down to do my business, I wondered how Clarence or anybody else had even found out about us, but truth be told the news could've leaked any number of ways. I remembered that there'd been plenty of other couples waiting to get married while we were there and it was possible that one of them or maybe even an employee of the chapel took a photo and shared it.

The mystery was officially solved though when I saw pictures of us plastered on an online tabloid site sent from both Denise and Simone. Denise's message read as surprised but still very congratulatory while Simone's…well…

I think you got this whole dump him and move on thing mixed up and I know you see your mama and daddy calling you!

I had indeed seen them calling back to back, but I figured there was no sense in answering until I had at least talked to Easton first about what we were going to do.

By the time I got to Mikel's message I'd almost cleared all of my notifications, but the way it punched me in the face I'd have preferred to get it out of the way much sooner.

Penny, what the hell is going on? Teegan just called me screaming about Easton wanting an annulment and putting you out of his room right now. Between this and your year-long hiatus, I think it's time we maybe reconsider this professional relationship. Call me when things calm down.

For a split second I thought he was joking, but sure enough in my email, there was a note from Teegan.

Ms. Pope,

I heard about the unfortunate event that took place in Las Vegas last night. Thankfully under such circumstances there should be no issues procuring an annulment, but for now it is in your best interest to vacate the premises immediately. As a precaution I will be sending a personal security team to check that you have departed by 1PM today. Rest assured, if you depart quietly we will ensure that you are taken care of financially for your emotional hardship.

Regards,
Teegan Ravin

To say that I was incensed would be an understatement. I felt like I was suddenly thrust into the middle of some wild soap opera plot and I couldn't understand how I had gotten there.

Last night had been so fun and magical and now it was going to cost me my career and potentially even get me arrested for trespassing. I would've taken Teegan's email as a bluff, but the fact that she'd already reached out to Mikel to twist the knife made things ten times worse.

I was foolish for even accepting the offer to work with Easton in the first place knowing the bad blood that I'd had with Teegan over Jake. Obviously she hadn't planned on us eloping, but she was crafty and sneaky so working with her in any capacity just gave her a chance to sabotage me and my career when an opportunity presented itself.

I felt like warmed-over poop that morning and maybe I deserved it. After what I'd been through with Jake I'd been so careless and naïve to think that I could enter this world again and come out unscathed.

When I emerged from the bathroom Easton was still pacing back and forth only now I noticed that he was shirtless and dressed in nothing but a pair of gray pajama pants. Even though I was mad as hell, I still felt a lick of desire tear through me. God, I was too thirsty for my own good sometimes.

"Look I'm not letting you do it like this, Teegan. We can still spin this and make it all go away without hurting Penny in the process," he said attempting to take up for me, but his words still hit me like a punch in the gut.

Yeah he was trying to be a good guy and make sure that I would be okay, but he'd pretty much confirmed that Teegan had still been right about him wanting the annulment. I was just a drunken mistake to him. A problem that he wanted to go away.

I suddenly felt a huge sob well up in my chest, but I shoved it right back down. I wasn't an idiot or a joke and I certainly wasn't going to cry over some man who didn't even want me once he'd sobered up. If there was one thing I'd learned from the last year, it was that no matter what I would always be okay. Later was as good a time as any to fall apart, but it couldn't happen now.

If it killed me I'd give Easton his annulment and maybe even take the money to literally make him pay for hurting my feelings. Maybe I'd donate it or invest it in the retreat or I could fly to LA and fling every cent of it in Teegan's smug face. Lucky for me I didn't have to decide now since they were all good options, but now my top priority was avoiding catching a charge for either murder or trespassing.

While Easton continued yapping away I took a quick shower then gathered my things.

I saw the manila envelope sitting on the nightstand and felt sadness creeping over me again, but I left it right where it sat. Easton could take care of it.

I looked around to see if I'd left anything behind and noticed something draped over the desk chair. Easton's black hoodie, the one he'd worn on our first date.

I ran my hands over it again, loving its softness, then lifted it up to my nose and smelled him in it. Maybe he'd been right about me all along, I thought as I pulled it over my head because I was officially claiming it as mine now and assuming my new identity as a hoodie thief.

On my way out Easton must've heard me opening the room door because that was when he came back inside and teasingly asked where *Mrs. Woods* was sneaking off to, but the cheeriness instantly left his face when he saw my packed bags.

"Actually, I think I'm gonna go with Pope-Woods," I told him in a tone that matched my hungover mood. "I'm not really into the whole patriarchy, ownership thing, you know?"

"Fine by me, but where are you going?" he asked in the softest voice I'd ever heard him use.

"I don't know. I hadn't really thought that far ahead yet, but with Teegan saying I needed to be out of here by one or get arrested for trespassing, I figured that I'd just get the easy part out of the way first."

"Wait what?!" he exclaimed suddenly regaining control of his voice's volume.

Through the phone I heard Teegan saying, "Easton, I can explain everything!" but he immediately ended the call and focused on me when he saw that I was heading out the door.

He begged me to come back inside so that we could get through all the apparent confusion together and like the fool I still was for him I agreed even though I had already heard the words directly from the horse's mouth.

"Penny, what are you talking about? Nobody is getting an annulment or arrested for trespassing. That is the most stupid thing...who even does that?" he asked incredulously and had the absolute nerve to still look confused.

He had to have been an even better actor than he'd given himself credit for before because I knew for a fact that he'd been in the loop long before I was and I was all caught up now.

"Easton, I just heard you tell Teegan to make your problem go away without hurting me and speaking of that, sorry, but you were too late. She already called my agent and now I probably won't have a career after this either!"

The room was quiet for a second except for my very heavy breathing as Easton took in my words.

"Okay first 'my problem' was all the press about the marriage and how it would affect your wish for privacy, **never** the marriage itself," he said as he pulled out his phone again. "And second I'm gonna get to the bottom of this thing with Teegan right now."

She barely let the phone ring once before practically screeching into the phone. "Easton, hello? Before you say anything, I need to tell you something about Penny first."

"Teegan, you're on speaker. Now you can tell me and my **wife** whatever the hell you'd like, but it better start with an explanation and an apology, not necessarily in that order."

His wife? My knees instantly wobbled a bit and I had to go sit down in a nearby chair.

In a cool tone with just a bit of a nervous tremble, Teegan replied, "Easton, I took the liberty of handling the situation myself. Like I told you before Penny has a reputation of being unstable so I wanted to ensure your safety by moving preemptively to resolve the situation."

"Unstable?!" I interjected once I'd heard enough. "You're the one who said that I would be paid well if I went away with no trouble. I'm guessing you were trying to set up some elaborate scheme to make it look like I was after his money or something, right?" I deduced since it was the only thing that made sense.

I was tired, hungover and my choked-back tears made my voice small, but I was still ready to go to war for what she was trying to pull. But fortunately or unfortunately for Teegan it wasn't me she had to be concerned about anymore.

Remember how Easton had been the picture of joy the night before? How his face had lit up and his eyes had sparkled? That was absolutely not what was happening now. If he could've ended Teegan through the phone, she would've been six feet under.

There was steel in his voice as he demanded an apology on my behalf.

She stuttered out, "I really don't think--"

"I will not repeat myself."

A pause, then a subdued, "I'm sorry for the miscommunication, Penny. I may have overstepped."

"That's Mrs. Pope-Woods to you and there's no 'may have' about it. You did overstep," he snarled. "My lawyer will be contacting you about severing our contract before the day is up and if you don't want your name to be in the headlines next you're also going to explain to Penny's agent how you made all this bullshit up in your head. And if I ever hear that you so much as frowned at the mention of any member of the Woods family, but especially Penny then the lawsuit coming your way will hit you so hard that your great-grandkids will feel it. Understand me?"

I looked at Easton—my husband!—like he was a hero.

Teegan's affronted huff warmed my battered little heart and she finally replied, "I understand. I'm sorry that things had to end up this way, Easton, but I'll work on those requirements immediately and once again, I apologize, Penny. Congrats on your nuptials and--" she began before I reached over and ended the call.

There was nothing left for her to say and I wanted to finally have a moment alone with my husband.

He tossed the phone onto the table then leaned against the wall. The silence was uncomfortable. The morass of emotions over the last twenty-four hours had drained me and he didn't look much better than I felt.

"Do you trust me, Penny?" he asked after a soul-releasing sigh.

I swallowed then stared at my hands. "Yes?"

"That sounded like a question."

"Easton, I had three different sources telling me that you wanted me gone, along with a possible arrest hanging over my head. You're rich and famous and I'm just…me."

He ran his fingers over his head and sighed. "Sounds like a perfect storm of shit."

"It was. And I've worked hard to rebuild my peace again and I won't let anybody take that from me."

"You mean like Jake and Teegan did?" he asked and I noted how weird it felt hearing him say his name. "I'm really sorry about all of this. I knew I should've gotten rid of her the second I heard about what she had done to you, but I guess I wanted to believe it was in the past since she had also been the one to bring you to me in the first place."

"When did you even find out about that?"

"Uh about a week ago when Denise told Amal. And you know I didn't believe him at first, but I hear she's a lot of fun when she lets her hair down."

"You guys talk about us to each other?" I asked because I'd made him swear not to tell a soul about us sneaking around, not even Elly.

"No of course not," he said unconvincingly. "Okay sometimes, but look I had to tell somebody! Holding in something this good was about to make me pop, woman!" he joked, but his love for me still infused every word.

Easton was so safe and worthy. Yes, I had doubted him at times because I was human., but unlike Jake he would always do his best to never hurt me.

I did have one more question though.

"Easton, what's the BAGG kit thing on the wedding chapel receipt?"

His smile went from saintly to sinister in record time.

"Oh. The bondage a go-go set. You forgot that I talked you into the Deluxe Lifetime Bondage ceremony?" he asked trying to contain his laughter. "Don't worry. We'll try that out later."

"Not on my honeymoon, you won't!" I said joining in on the joke with him.

"Honeymoon, huh? I think I like the sound of that," he said as he pushed up off the wall then approached me. "Because I don't plan on leaving this room for the rest of this weekend, Penny, maybe even the next week. I want to have you in so many ways that you don't have the energy to doubt anything about us again. You're mine and I'm yours, okay?"

He had been serious in the delivery of his previous words,

but he finally cracked a smile again when he noticed what I was wearing.

"You were about to leave and steal my hoodie, weren't you?"

"Maybe." He swept me up into his arms then started walking towards the bed.

"Good thing I caught you then, huh?" He caressed my face, traced my lips then looked at me with wonder. "I meant every word I said last night, Penny. I love you so much and I can't wait to spend the rest of my life with you."

"So that alcohol was like a truth serum for you then? Is that what you're saying?"

"I'd like to think that it was, but let's be honest. You know we were gonna get married eventually anyway. It was just a question of when."

He laid me down on the bed then busied himself taking off my clothes and shoes. I was putty in his hands so I just laid there and let him do it and soon enough I was down to nothing but my skin and a blush.

"You sound pretty sure of yourself." I stretched and purred under Easton's hands as he touched me all over, learning me, memorizing everything.

"I mean, if you hadn't said yes, I would've just followed my dad's footsteps and stolen you away to our island." He laid down beside me and peppered soft kisses all over my exposed flesh. "If it worked for him, there's no reason it couldn't work for me, right?"

Just before his lips touched mine he gripped my hand in his, our rings catching the light of the early afternoon sun.

"Yeah except you wouldn't have to steal me," I told him honestly. "I love you, *Earl* Easton Woods Jr., from the bottom of my heart and back."

"I'm gonna hold you to that, Mrs. Pope-Woods. That's a promise."

His kiss felt different this time. It wasn't the lusty coupling of lips and tongue like in the solarium. This was a sweet, persuasive kiss that felt like Easton was pleading his case to me. I accepted him wholeheartedly, holding him

close and giving him everything I
had.

Leaning up over me, he
traced lines all over my body,
massaging me, touching
everything with almost a
reverent attentiveness, his level
of urgency suddenly more
intense.

"I've never seen you in the
daylight like this. You're like an
angel."

"You're not so bad yourself," I
said as my hand wandered lower
and rested on his abs, tracing
them with my finger. "You and
your twenty abs."

Without warning he rolled
us over then sat me directly on
top of his face. The position was
intense and he held on so tightly
that I couldn't do anything but sit

there on his mouth and lose my mind.

"Easton," I groaned as I felt my orgasm welling up, "I don't think I can hold back anymore."

"So don't," he said simply into my body.

That was all I need to hear and a few seconds later I was crying out as the orgasm hit me in a mad sweep of sensation, making me buck even harder. As I came down from the rush, he suddenly caught my hips, positioned me on top of him then drove me down onto his full length with a demanding thrust of his hips.

He gripped my hips as I continued to crash through my orgasm, guiding me up and down his whole thickness in a continual wave of movement. He impaled me over and over again forcing me to shudder at the sensation and nearly lose myself in our joined bodies.

I wasn't out of tricks though. A horse girl all my life, I was built for this and he was just a different type of stallion.

Before he could respond I caught his hands in mine and trapped them over his head. I swiveled my hips and started to get to work, toying with him and reveling in his sighs and moans.

"Penny," Easton hissed then gritted his teeth and tried to take back control again, but I wouldn't let him. "Fuck. You're gonna kill me."

All that did was encourage me and made me giddy-up with more gusto than before. In fact, my head started to loll back and forth as I was so completely sunken into pleasure that I lost track of what I was doing.

Easton took advantage of my grip loosening on his hands then flipped me on my back again. I yelped as he suddenly pistoned in and out of me, hitting my clit and making me explode for a second time. After a moment he joined me, groaning out his release and collapsing on top of me with his head on my bosom.

After our hearts had safely settled back into our chests, I curled into him and prepared to surrender to sleep, but he began speaking and jolted me back awake.

"I'm really embarrassed to say this and I'll deny it if you ever tell anybody, but the other day I heard a Taylor Swift song that made me think about you."

"Uh oh." He grinned widely then assured me that it wasn't from her revenge era. "Wait just how many Taylor Swift eras are you familiar with, Easton?" I asked him curiously then went on to tease him as he tried to deny being a proud Swiftie like I was.

The conversation naturally flowed into what music artists he wasn't ashamed to claim publicly and eventually ended with him drifting off almost midsentence because he was so exhausted. I kissed his sleeping face then made a mental note to ask him the name of the song later even though I had a feeling I knew which one he'd meant.

Because just like his hoodies and my favorite black nail polish, deep down I knew that we would never go out of style either.

WE NEVER GO OUT OF STYLE

FOLLOW ME

Thanks for reading! If you don't want to miss out on any updates about future works of mine then find me on all social media platforms as TanSaidWhat, sign up for my mailing list and join my reading group Turning The Page With Tanzania Glover.

Visit www.tanzaniaglover.com

And if the cover art took your breath away as much as it did mine, check out the talented artist Sia Tania! Thank you so much for bringing this couple to life!